Great Gray

A Book about Exceeding "No Expectations"

Written by
Beverly Davis

Bev Davis '16

Illustrations by
Linda Cowen

References for names and terminology:
www.indianhindunames.com
www.thefreedictionary.com

First Edition 2014
Published in the USA by *thewordverve inc.* (www.thewordverve.com)

eBook ISBN: 978-1-941251-04-1
Paperback ISBN: 978-1-941251-05-8

Library of Congress Control Number: 2014934265

Great Gray

A Book with Verve by *thewordverve inc.*

Cover and interior artwork by Linda Cowen
www.lindacowen.weebly.com

Cover and interior design by Robin Krauss
http://www.bookformatters.com

Ebook formatting by Bob Houston
http://facebook.com/eBookFormatting

DEDICATION

To my children, Kristen and Gavin Rehfeldt

My loving and supportive husband Steve

And in memory of Eileen Fay

Peace and blessings.

The beautiful Saguna* and the powerful Prabir*, two respected elephants in the Indian village called Anupam, were anticipating the birth of their first calf.

The expectant Saguna had waited a long time for this event. She dreamed of her perfect calf. They would parade proudly throughout the tropical forest showing off their little one.

Prabir, the proud papa, was planning many things he would teach his son. Of course, it would be a male, and he would teach him to hunt and knock down trees, making way for buildings and roads.

---

* The name Saguna means virtuous.
* The name Prabir means hero, brave one.

His greatest dream for his son would be to carry the Maharajah Anupam* in festivals. This honor, passed from the baby's grandfather, was now his honor. He would teach his son to strut with his ears wide and forward. His back would be covered in jewels, his tusks covered in gold.

He would be the most beautiful elephant with the proudest father. They would name him Atul*, after his great-grandfather, because there would never be another elephant such as him.

---

* Maharajah means great king. Maharajah Anupam means King of Anupam.

* The name Atul means matchless.

For twenty-two months, the couple dreamt about what life would be like when their two-hundred-pound bundle of joy arrived.

His perfectly shaped ears would not exceed the height of his neck, and his hearing would be especially good. They would teach him how to use his trunk as a straw to squirt water into his mouth.

Santosh*, the young mahout*, would spend twenty-six days of the month with their son as he began to train him to wear the vahana* on his back. The boy would bathe their son and teach him to cool his blood in the great jungle by fanning his ears. Yes, everything was ready.

---

* The name Santosh means happiness.

* A mahout is a keeper and driver of the elephant.

* A vahana is a vehical or carrier, in this case that sits atop the elephant.

The great day arrived, and Saguna was surrounded by the female elephants as she began to give birth. Everything went well. But as the baby was being readied to meet his papa, they noticed something was not quite right.

Yes, he was a boy. Their son had four legs and soft, brownish-gray skin with small tufts of hair. His trunk was absolutely perfect, the perfect length for this absolutely perfect calf!

But as they began to unfurl his baby ears, the elephant named Sneh* said, "Oh dear."

Saguna scrunched her brow. "Oh dear, what?"

"There seems to be something not quite right with his ears," Sneh said.

"How can that be?" Saguna questioned. "He's perfect in every way."

"Well, here . . . look!"

His mother stared at her newborn, surprised at what she saw.

---

* The name Sneh means love.

Yes, it was true. He did have two perfect ears. His right ear was where it should be—on the right side of his head—but the other ear rose on *top of his head.*

The female elephants tried and tried again to straighten this ear and bring it around to the left side of his head.

"It must be twisted," said his mother.

"Let's hold it down with these stones; I'm sure that's all it will need," said Sneh.

They pushed the ear to the left and weighed it down with several flat stones.

BOING!

The ear went back to its original position, like a little flag on a mast.

"Oh, my goodness, what will we do? His father is waiting impatiently to see him," said his mother.

"I've got an idea. We'll cover his ears with this long, silk cloth. Maybe it will just take a little time and the ear will fall into its proper place," encouraged Sneh.

The two female elephants took the little one, wrapped him in silk, and then presented him to his father.

"What a perfect calf my son is," said Prabir with joy. "He will walk proudly with the maharajah on his back."

Just as he said that, the little elephant's silk wrapping opened . . . and out popped his ear.

"What is this?" Prabir said as he stared at the ear perched on top of his son's head. "This will never do."

"We're sure it will settle down. Look at him; he is perfect in every other way," Saguna reassured her husband.

"He'll never be able to carry the maharajah. Bah, he'll never amount to anything," his father trumpeted.

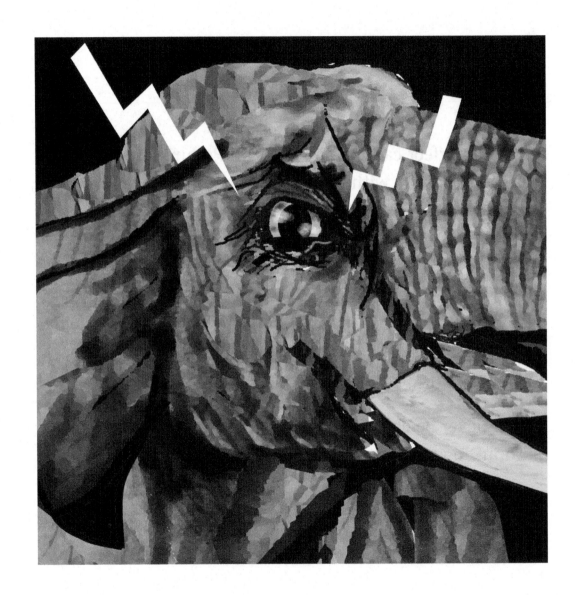

"Poor little Atul," cried Sneh.

"Atul! His name will not be Atul! That name will be saved for our next son, our perfect son," Prabir shouted.

"What shall we name him then? He must have a name," cried the calf's mother.

"I don't care. That thing looks like a gray flag on top of his head. Just call him Gray."

Little Gray was led into the tropical forest with his mahout, Santosh.

But instead of learning how to carry the great maharajah and being covered with jewels, he was carrying buckets of water and pushing tree trunks along the forest floor.

Given to a contractor hired to build a resort on the edge of the beautiful, dense tropical forest, Gray had to clear the land.

All the other elephants and their mahouts made fun of Gray.

"What's that growing out of your head? Is that a flag waving? No, that's your ear," they taunted.

This made Gray very sad, and Santosh very angry.

"We'll show them," Santosh yelled. He picked up several rocks and using Gray's ear as a catapult, sailed them over the trees at the mean mahouts.

"Hey, where are those coming from?" the others cried.

"We showed them, didn't we, Gray?"

Suddenly, Gray's ear waved "yes."

"Gray, did you just wave yes?" Santosh said, astonished.

The ear flapped forward and backward again.

"Gray, that's great. I know none of those fools over there can do that."

Gray's ear waved forward and backward and then side to side.

"This is pretty amazing, Gray, but let's keep it to ourselves for the time being. It will be our secret."

Gray flapped his ear in agreement.

Many weeks passed. Gray and Santosh continued to keep their secret.

During the day, they would go about the forest moving trees and pulling roots, as they made room for new buildings.

At night, Santosh would teach Gray the flag semaphore system*, a code that sailors used before radio transmission. He taught Gray from a book he found long ago near the harbor.

"The book says that each movement of two flags designates a letter in the alphabet. But instead of using two flags, we'll use your two ears," Santosh said excitedly.

After many months of practice, Gray could spell out any word Santosh requested by the twitch of his two giant ears.

---

* The flag semaphore alphabet is at the back of this book.

One bright and sunny day when they were rolling barrels of water from the sea, Gray heard a great rumbling, a rumbling like nothing he had ever heard.

It came from far away under the sea.

He stopped and listened, then stopped and listened again.

"What's wrong, Gray? What do you hear?" Santosh called. He knew an elephant's hearing was quite good, and with Gray's one ear on top of his head . . . well, Santosh figured Gray could hear better than any other elephant around.

Suddenly Gray's ears began to twitch and twist, spelling out these words: TROUBLE! TROUBLE!

His ears waved back and forth.

"Trouble from the sea?" Santosh asked.

Back and forth, Santosh read.

"If there's trouble, we have to save everyone."

Santosh yelled to all who could hear him, "Get back from the water! There's trouble. Get back!"

Gray, with Santosh on his back, began to stampede from the edge, followed by the other elephants.

"What's the rush? I don't hear anything," one of the mean mahouts said.

But Gray felt trouble under the water, and Santosh trusted Gray's instincts.

"Don't ask questions, just head for the inland mountains," said Santosh.

The herd of elephants stampeded into the mountains with their mahouts on their backs, as a wall of water hit the shore with a force of a thousand elephants.

The area that had been cleared for construction was under the raging tide.

"We would have been under that water if it hadn't been for Gray's great hearing and special talent," said the head of the construction crew.

"Hooray for Gray!" shouted everyone.

"Hooray for Great Gray! For there has never been another elephant such as him!"

Eventually, word of Great Gray's heroics reached the Maharajah Anupam.

"The festival is tomorrow, and Great Gray will carry me," Maharajah Anupam announced. "And as a show of my gratitude, he will also carry my son."

The day arrived, and never was there a day like it. The entire town joined in the celebration to honor Great Gray because he saved so many people.

Great Gray was covered in jewels, his tusks were covered in gold, and his ears shaded the son of the Maharajah from the bright sun.

Also at the parade were Gray's parents. When Gray passed them, he gave them a wink as his ears twitched several times, spelling out this word: LOVE.

His parents beamed with pride.

MESSAGE FROM THE AUTHOR

Ten years ago, after a lifetime seeking greater purpose for my life, I realized a call to serve God. So at the age of fifty-four, I left my career as a successful interior designer, sold my home, and began seminary in Chicago, my hometown.

The fact that I was accepted is unique in itself, but the fact that I am now an ordained pastor in the United Church of Christ is an example that God is never finished with us, ever.

A little over four years ago, as I was beginning to adjust to my new life in a new place, I had a dream. At first, I thought it was just a silly fantasy, but as I reflected and processed, I realized it was about me. It was my life!

Even though I have had disappointment in my life and sometimes didn't have much value in myself or my talents, I know God has carried me. He continues to guide me in my journey of faith.

Just like little Gray and so many others, it took God to open my eyes to see my potential and how to share and encourage others.

And just like Gray carried the maharajah and his son in the parade, I served a small church until 2013 in North Central Wisconsin, a long way from my roots on the south side of Chicago and my former career as an interior designer. I am currently living in Milwaukee with my husband Steve and our dog Coco. I am now a hospice chaplain.

Gray and I are one and the same. I suspect there are a lot of other "Grays" out there as well. I hope my little story of exceeding "no expectations" will help others see their worth and the value God puts on their lives.

—Reverend Beverly Davis

FLAG SEMAPHORE SYSTEM

(the alphabet)

CPSIA information can be obtained
at www.ICGtesting.com
Printed in the USA
LVOW03s2232270816

502140LV00001B/2/P

9 781941 251058